TRAIN TRIP

Written by
Deanna Caswell

Illustrated by
Dan Andreasen

Disney • HYPERION BOOKS

New York

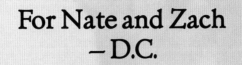

For Nate and Zach
— D.C.

For Katrina
— D.A.

Clear sky. Noon heat.
Sit and wait. Wiggly feet.

Ticket ready. Tight grip.
To Grandma's house. Train trip!
Gleaming giant. Endless track.
Long pants. Knapsack.

Capped conductor. Dark suit.
Polished buttons. Crisp salute.
Steel steps. People squeeze.
Cloth seats. "Tickets, please!"

"All aboard!" Tummy leaps.
Whistle blows. Engine creeps.

Mounting speed. Leaving town.
Spirits high. Windows down.

Grain fields. Busy plows.
Sloping pastures. Blurry cows.

Rumbling, rocking, humming tracks.
"Are we there yet?" Munching snacks.

Switching seats. Counting miles.
*Chuff*ing up and down the aisles.

Shoulder tap. "Follow me."
"Where to?" "You'll see."

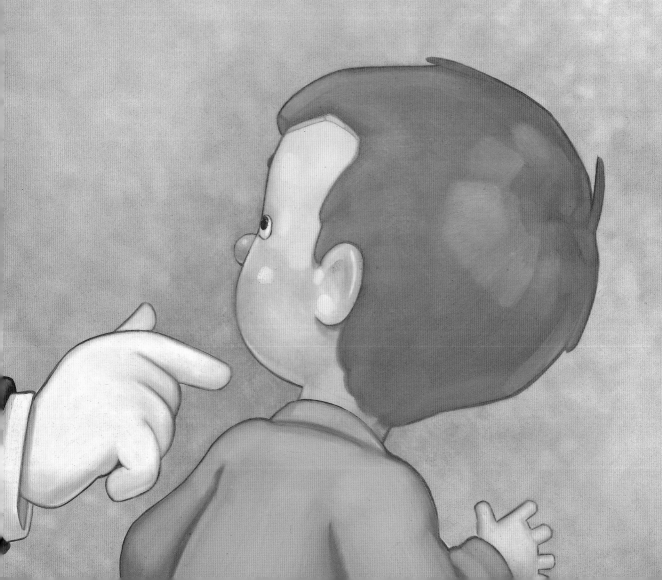

WHOOOOO-WHOOOOO!

Open door. Peek inside.
Buttons, gauges. Eyes wide.
Special treat. "Come on in!"
"Sound the whistle?" Eager grin.

Tiny towns whizzing by.
Tunnels, bridges, hours fly.

Sun sets. Squinting, peering.
Pinpricked darkness. City nearing!

Buildings loom. Engine slows.
Destination. Station glows.

"Next stop . . . !" Gather things.
Platform full. Bell rings.

Disembark. Scan the crowd.
Laughter, greetings. Voices loud.
Over there! Favorite face.
Pearls and curls. Warm embrace.

Hand in hand. Chug away.
Can't wait to drive a train someday!